Little PEOPLE Angel Book

ISBN 978-1-64416-568-3 (paperback)
ISBN 978-1-09800-035-6 (hardcover)
ISBN 978-1-64416-569-0 (digital)

Christian Faith Publishing, Inc.
832 Park Avenue
Meadville, PA 16335
www.christianfaithpublishing.com

Printed in the United States of America

To my special and wonderful stepdaughter
Chelsey Ynostrosa

Contents

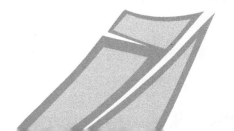

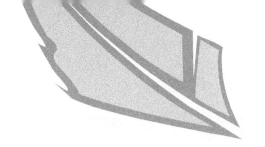

God Is

God is all-loving, all-knowing and loves us no matter what.

If we are good, He is very pleased and very happy!

Honesty, kindness, loyalty, and being helpful are several of many good behaviors.

If we misbehave, He is very sad. He never wants to hurt us, and He never would want us to hurt anyone else.

Hitting, being hurtful, stealing, lying, or cheating are a few of the many bad behaviors.

God gives us a choice; this is called *free will.*

It is up to us to decide if we want to be good or bad.

God is:

All-Powerful, good, and perfect.

God made man, women, children, plants, trees, animals, birds, fish, dogs, cats, stars, the moon, sun, land, mountains, lakes, rivers, water, waterfalls, earth, and all planets.

God made everyone and everything, and God made even *you*!

God is so amazing and full of love and energy. His light is so bright that it would hurt our eyes to look at Him;

so He made for us the angels.

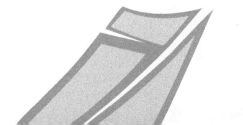

Angels Are

Angels are messengers from God.

They are God's helpers created to help us. They always speak the "Truth" and would never say bad things to us, tell us bad things, or expect us to do anything bad.

They only speak with "love and understanding."

And angels will always help us, but we must remember to ask them, and they love it when we thank them!

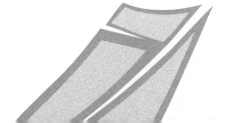

Angels are mostly invisible, but they can become anyone, any shape, or any form. They will never scare us or hurt us.

Angels are full of love, peace, and happiness.

Angels love us, and they always want to help us.

There are many types of angels.

One of the most common one is your *guardian angel.*

Then there are your *mighty archangels.*

Guardian Angels

Everyone has a guardian angel with them since birth and stays with you until you go to heaven. In the meanwhile, they follow you around to help you make the right decisions.

They love you and stay with you so you are never alone.

"Angel Prayer" to your guardian angel:

Angel of God,
My guardian dear,
To whom his love
Commits me here,
Ever this day
Be at my side,
To light and guard,
To rule and guide.
Amen.

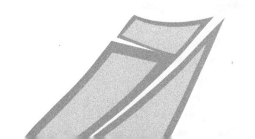

Archangels

rchangels are the most powerful angels.

They can do anything! They can protect us from harm. But you have to ask for their help and you must *believe!*

Archangel Michael is God's right hand. He is the *highest archangel* who sits next to God. He helps all the rest of the angels who help us. That is his job; you might say he is the "Boss Angel."

There are so many archangels. Here are just few to mention:

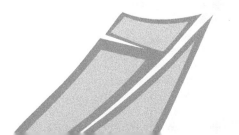

Archangel Uriel: If you are confused, he will help you to see things clearly.

Archangel Raphael: Will help you to heal if you are sick.

Archangel Gabriel: He loves to deliver messages from God and helps you to communicate, helps you with writing, speaking truthfully, and acting honestly.

Archangel Azrael: He surrounds grieving and dying persons with his bright light, to bring them comfort, happiness, and freedom from suffering. He is known as "The Angel of Death."

Archangel Ariel: She helps us to be strong and gives us confidence and encouragement.

There are so many angels that if you look up at the sky and see all the stars… It is said that every star has at least a million angels for "every star!"

So never be afraid to ask the angels for help and remember… You are never alone! God bless you!

And always be kind to people because you never know…

They might be an "Angel in Disguise!"

Little Reminders

If you laugh, the world laughs with you! If you cry, you cry alone.

If you are moody, sad, or being difficult…

People won't want to be around you…

You will be lonely!

Poem: Anonymous

So, If you have done a good deed…no one knows but you… Remember, God sees everything, and is pleased with what you do!

Tools for Helping You When You Get Angry

When you are angry, there is a "reason." You might be afraid, mad, sad, scared, hurt, fearful, upset, frustrated, or disappointed. A lot of times, people are unaware of your feelings and would never want to hurt you or make you angry.

Here are some suggestions on what to do when you feel angry or when you feel that you are going to lose your temper:

1. Admit that you are angry ("I'm feeling angry because… I am afraid, mad, sad, scared…").
2. Ask your angels to help you to understand what is going on. Ask yourself, "Why am I feeling, afraid, mad, sad, scared…?"
3. Don't blame others for your behavior.
4. Take five deep breaths.
5. Sometimes it is hard to figure it out. You can always talk to the angels; they will always listen with a loving heart. They will never judge you.
6. You can draw pictures of what is going on.
7. Sing to them.
8. Write a letter to them. (You can use your own words to help describe your feelings.)
9. Exercise: run, jump rope, and dance, or anything to help you release your anger.
10. When you finally calm down, tell the person that you are sorry for your anger and explain your "true feelings."
11. Give yourself a "hug" and "thank the angels for their help."
12. Let go, move on, and remember that *God* is all-loving and always forgives us!

So try to be:

Happy always
Friendly to everyone
Find the good in all you meet
Be honest and caring
Always truthful
Love your family
And
Trust your angels,
They are always and forever there for you, for guidance,
For advice
And for
Never ending *love*.
The End

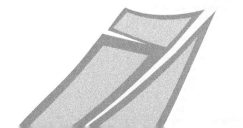

Acknowledgments

I would like to Thank everyone who helped me write this *"Little People, Angel Book."*

First and foremost, having learned to connect with my angels through prayer, meditation, and the power of love, is what guided me while writing this book.

To my husband of twenty-four years, Chuck, who at first called himself, "An open-minded skeptic."

He now believes in God, the power of prayers, and angels.

To my first husband, Bill, who is in Heaven and keeps sending angels my way.

My sisters Mary and Lucina, brothers Joe and Jeff, who have been kind enough to listen to my many angel experiences.

To my dearest friends and believers Diane, Linda, Sarah, Jana, Karen, Chelsea, Gina, Joyce, Tim, Tom, and Dave, who have helped me through life and gave me pointers on the writing of this *"Little People, Angel Book."* To my folks Eleanor and Tom, who had an amazing blind faith in GOD!

Mostly, I would like to thank my stepdaughter Chelsey, for asking me to write this book for her daughter, Bella.

Bella was having some difficulties and needed some spiritual guidance, which her parents and this book provided.

I especially would like to thank all those that believe in angels and power of God!

Thank you all!

I couldn't have done it without you!

In Loving Memory
Our Dear Friend
Tim Egan

About the Author

The author Ginny Prokop has been a waitress in a casino in Lake Tahoe for forty-three years. She loves people and her job. She believes that we are all connected to each other, and we all have a piece of God's heart in us! Ginny is a simple person. She loves to make people happy, and that is what makes her most complete as a person.